Chateau de Paix

Chateau de Paix

Nightmare Hiding in Paradise

R. C. JETTE

RESOURCE *Publications* • Eugene, Oregon

Resource Publications
An Imprint of Wipf and Stock Publishers
199 W. 8th Ave., Suite 3
Eugene, OR 97401

www.wipfandstock.com

PAPERBACK ISBN: 978-1-7252-8172-1
HARDCOVER ISBN: 978-1-7252-8171-4
EBOOK ISBN: 978-1-7252-8173-8

Manufactured in the U.S.A.   08/12/20

All Scripture references are taken from the King James Version (KJV): KING JAMES VERSION, public domain.

THIS BOOK IS DEDICATED to my Lord Jesus Christ who makes the impossible possible by faith, my husband (Paul) who has been by my side through thick and thin, my son (PJ) his daughter (Kierra), my daughter (Dawn) who has freed me up to write, my daughter (Christina) her sons (Andrew, Matthew, Joshua) and her daughter (Sarah) who is with the Lord, Susanna and Mike who have been such a help, and to all who have influenced my life throughout the years.

My special thanks is given to Wipf and Stock Publishers for their continued publication of my books under their Resource Publications. I thank their staff who have constantly made this challenge more tolerable. I am grateful to Joe Delahanty, Jim Tedrick, Joshua Little, Ian Creeger, and Stephanie Randels. Special mention is given to Matthew Wimer, George Callihan, Shannon Carter, Savanah Landerholm, and Rachel Saunders to whom words cannot convey my gratitude.

For nothing is secret, that shall not be made manifest; neither any thing hid, that shall not be known and come abroad (Luke 8:17).

And we know that all things work together for good to them that love God, to them who are the called according to his purpose (Romans 8:28).

Contents

Prologue

A RAVEN SOARS THROUGH the moonlight. Behind him, stands a gothic mansion silent and foreboding like a mysterious dark secret. From the raven's vantage point is an old Oak tree below. As he descends towards it, the moonlight reveals the tree is centered in what appears to be a medieval garden with high walls. It is in full bloom with sweet bay, sweet myrtle, rosemary, sage, thyme, and beds of fennel, cabbage, onions, garlic, leeks, radishes, etc.

Strategically placed are almond, apple, cherry, fig, hazelnut, mulberry, pear, and plum trees. Red roses are planted near the South wall. Near each of the four corners of the wall is a statue of an ancient Hindu god positioned as if ready for war.

In the north corner is a statue of Brahma with his four heads and four arms. In the south corner stands a statue of Vishnu with his blue human body and four hands. Shiva with his human body, blue face and neck is situated in the west corner. Lastly, in the east corner is the goddess Durga with her eight hands carrying weapons of various kinds and riding a lion.

As the raven gets closer to the tree, a young woman, sitting on a bench under the tree comes into focus. Her pale complexion and long black hair seem to give her a bewitching appearance as she appears to be staring at one of the ancient statues that resembles a woman riding on a lion.

The raven, unnoticed by the woman, lands on the branch above her. Behind her two dark figures step out of the shadows and startle her. They smile, and recognition comforts her. The female offers her a nightcap. She takes the glass, the female and male join her in the drink.

Prologue

The young woman realizes that something is wrong when she can no longer focus in her surroundings. As she struggles to stand up, she falls down to the sinister laughter of the male. When she awakens, she is in a foreign environment with prison bars.

Chapter One

The Water Cooler

"THAT WATER COOLER IS beginning to be an adversary most formidable," Margaret mumbled as she went to sit at a table in the company cafeteria. She sighed heavily, set her tray down on the table, placed her pocketbook down, pulled out a book from inside, and sat down.

She held her book in her left hand and started to eat her low-calorie meal with her right hand. As she took a sip of her diet cola, she feels her blood boil as she views Carlotta heading for the water cooler. "If Joel comes in and goes to the cooler, I do believe I'm going to confront them both."

"Hey," a voice next to her said. "Are you so overworked that you've begun to talk to yourself?" Titus smiled and gestured to the seat opposite her. "Do you mind if I sit here?"

"Of course not," Margaret said. "But I guess I am talking to myself." She rubbed the back of her neck with her right hand. "To be honest, I'm not sure what's going on with your brother."

"Joel?" His eyebrows squished together. "He's an open book. I've known him since I was ten. That's twenty-eight years, and my brother has never been anything but open and honest." He gave a throaty laugh. "Of course, there were times when people didn't believe this black guy was his brother. But when the Schneider's adopted me at eight and brought me to America from Liberia, I know God can do anything."

Margaret's blue eyes looked at him with sadness. "I thought God could do anything, but I don't know what to think now." She giggled. "Sorry about that. I'm still trying to figure out why God didn't heal my mother." She sighed. "As for Joel, he seems to be paying a lot of attention to Carlotta lately." She nodded towards the water cooler. "She looks like a fashion model."

Titus pulled his right eyebrow with his right thumb and forefinger. "Margaret, Joel has been in love with you since you were in the Youth Group at church." His eyebrows squished together. "Seriously, I think you should've taken time out of work after your mother died last month. According to Ecclesiastes there is a time to mourn. People need time to heal from such a loss. As a matter of fact, Joel has been concerned about you."

She shrugged her shoulders. "I'm fine. I believe work keeps me busy and my mind off the grief." She giggled. "Besides, I'm almost at the level for a nice bonus this year." She paused as her peripheral vision viewed Joel walking towards the water cooler.

Joel glanced her way, but Margaret pretended she didn't see him. "Watch. See what I mean," she whispered to Titus.

Titus glanced towards Joel and saw Carlotta slip a note into his hand. As Joel read the note, they both grinned at each other.

"That's what I've witnessed almost daily for some time now. There's clearly something going on." She gestured with her right hand. "Do I go over there and confront them? Do I just give him back his engagement ring? How can I ignore what's happening before my very eyes?"

"Have you asked him about it?"

"Of course! " She rubbed the back of her neck with her right hand. "Well, not right out. I just mentioned how beautiful Carlotta was to see his reaction." She gestured with both hands. "He just said the only beautiful one to him was me."

"There. I'm sure there's a good explanation to this water cooler thing." He gave a wide grin. "I think we need to wait and see what Joel is doing." He patted her right hand. "Believe me, if there was something, he would've mentioned it to me. We've had a David and Jonathan relationship since he was about six or so."

Margaret placed her long black hair behind her ears with both hands. "I'll heed your counsel and see what's what." Her blue eyes widened. "But what if he hasn't said anything to you because he doesn't want to be reprimanded?" She gestured with her right hand. "What if he's waiting for the right moment to break the engagement?"

Titus gave a throaty laugh. "Margaret, Margaret, Margaret! What's happening to you? I've never seen you so insecure. You must trust the Lord and quit leaning on your own understanding." He paused. "My brother has never done an underhanded thing in his life. It's not his nature to be deceitful." He pulled his right eyebrow with his right thumb and forefinger. "I'm not trying to seem controlling, but please pray about taking some time to grieve your mother's death." He gazed into her eyes. "You feel like you're in a dark tunnel, but the light is at the end. Your grief has you seeing only darkness." He patted her right hand. "You must trust the Lord to take you through to the light."

"I must admit it does seem quite dark at present. Perhaps, Joel isn't God's choice for me. Perhaps, I chose him and not God."

Titus patted her right hand. "Margaret, Joel prayed this through. The Lord made certain that you are his wife." He paused. "Now, I may be ten years older than my brother, but God hasn't pointed out my wife yet. She must be a woman after God's own heart." He sat back and laughed. "At first. I thought I was asking a tall order from the Lord. But he calmed me by saying that desire had been put there by him. It's a preventative so I don't marry before he brings his foreordained wife into my life."

Before she could respond, she felt a hand on her right shoulder. "Are you enjoying this beautiful day the Lord has made?" Joel said. "All I know is that I thought I'd never get that job done." He gave a heavy sigh. "I'm delighted that it's almost finished. It's been quite the ordeal."

She rubbed the back of her neck with her right hand. "What job?" Her blue eyes widened. "I didn't know you were having trouble with anything."

Joel scratched the back of his head with his right hand. "It doesn't seem like anything now." He clasped his hands together. "Thank God, it's about complete." He pulled out a chair and sat next to Margaret. "What book are you reading?"

"The Mysteries of Udolpho."

Titus gave out a throaty laugh. "Well, I pray you don't become overwhelmed like Emily in the story." He patted her right hand. "I'm not sure that's a story to read after just losing your mother."

Joel's eyebrows squished together. "I think my brother might have a point there. That is quite the story with Emily losing her mother, her father, trying to understand her Aunt's death, and all the mystery about Montoni."

Margaret giggled. "You two are being ridiculous. I chose this book, because I just wanted to get into some gothic place away from everything." She gestured with her right hand. "One of the nurses who tended to my mother told me how she couldn't put it down. It was as though Emily was in paradise. After her mother dies, she and her father go on a journey. After his death, she finds herself in a nightmare of the horrors of Udolpho." She gave a sigh. "It seemed like the perfect book explaining what I've been feeling."

Joel took her right hand and held it between both his hands. "Margaret, only the Lord can give comfort during this time. You've missed church for several weeks." His brown eyes gazed at her. "Your mother never missed church. I do wish you would seriously take time to grieve before the grief consumes you."

Margaret threw up both hands. "What it is with you two? I'm fine. I told you I missed church because I couldn't sit there without my mother. I'm healing in my way." She paused. "Just give me a little more time."

Joel kissed her forehead. "I've been praying for you. I know you'll come through. The Lord promises that when we love him, all things we go through will work together for our good." He scratched the back of his head with his right hand. "We may not see any good in it, but faith says God will bring about something good. He is faithful to his word."

Titus gave a wide grin. "I do believe Joel is correct. For I have a strong feeling that something good is going to come out of this grief." He touched her right hand. "I don't mean that it's good that your mother died, but God has a way of making something good come out of our trials. There is light at the end of the tunnel." He paused and looked into her eyes. "We have to trust in his love for us." He paused. "You must get your eyes off your grief and onto him. Remember, that's how Peter sunk. He walked on the water while keeping his eyes on Jesus, but sunk when he looked away at the storm."

Margaret fought back tears. "That's what my mother told me."

Chapter Two

Storms Rage Within and Without

A TURBULENT SENSIBILITY RACED through Margaret as she peered out her living room window. Her emotions smoldered like an active volcano ready to spew out molting lava as she watched Hurricane Vastare rampage outside. Winds chanted the ritual of destruction, leaves whirled like musical tops spun out of control. Near the garden, the old elm tree, forced to genuflect before the power of the storm appeared to supplicate for its safety.

As she witnessed the tree arch humbler and humbler, fear took control of her emotions. Suddenly her being mingled with the tree, and she became one with it in the struggle to survive. Margaret felt them both being plucked up by the giant tendrils of some unknown force of destruction.

She grabbed her head with both hands, closed her eyes, and tried to focus on reality. Sensing a need to recover her reasoning, she opened her eyes to gaze at the tree. With its limbs stretched towards heaven, it seemed to laugh as it danced to the song of the wind.

Margaret opened her briefcase and searched frantically for the vacation pamphlet. The daily grief had her strung out like a coil ready to snap. She sat down in the bow back Windsor arm chair that was her mother's. "God! Why didn't you heal her? Your word says, that faith the size of mustard seed can remove mountains. I know I believed." She grit her teeth together. "You took my father before I even knew him. You took my mother, and now you are taking Joel. You take everyone I love."

The tears streamed down her face. "Now, I have to watch Joel and Carlotta at the water cooler." At the thought of seeing them caused a spasmodic trembling within. "What do they think I am? I must appear like a fool. As if I don't see them passing notes back and forth." She gave a heavy sigh. "I hardly know Carlotta, but my fiancé has been too evasive of late. I sense his next move is to call off the wedding." She rubbed the back of her neck with her right hand. "Even Titus has seen them passing notes." She grabbed her head with both hands. "I know what Titus said, but I don't know how much longer I can follow his counsel."

"I have to find that brochure," Margaret said emptying her briefcase on the maple drop-leaf coffee table." She sighed heavily. "I have to find it. I'm beginning to believe Titus is right. I do need to get away. When I get back, I'll beat Joel to the punch and call the wedding off." She paused. "Who am I kidding? Joel is all I have left." She looked at the bronze cross hanging on the wall over a camel back couch. "Why do you take everyone I love?"

She sat back and with both hands on her head. "God help me! Am I going shipwreck. I know I saw the tree almost topple over. I know I've seen them passing notes." She paused. "Titus saw them passing the note. I know I am not imagining things. But the tree doesn't seem to be affected at all by the storm."

"I need to get away." Margaret sighed, heavily. "Where is that brochure?" Her eyes focused on the papers on the coffee table. "There it is." She immediately picked it up and her eyes began to read the words. "Does daily stress have you undone? Come away for two glorious weeks of nothing." She drops her right hand and the leaflet to her lap. She then stretches out her left hand to view her diamond ring surrounded by sapphires. As she sits back, tears stroll down her cheeks as a picture of Joel receiving a note from Carlotta at the water cooler flashes through her mind.

She wiped her eyes and continues to read the brochure. "Two beautiful weeks at the Chateau de Paix is what you need. Splendid scenery and gothic chateau will calm the nerves of anyone."

Margaret perceived two weeks of peace and tranquility would be like a blissful experience at present. "That's it," she said. "I'll do it." She sat back and folded her arms. "I'll make reservations with the chateau and then set up everything with the airline. Then I'll obtain the time off from work on Monday and work until I can leave for the chateau."

Once she made the reservations and secured her flight, she knew she would leave on Friday night. Now, to make it through the next week at work. She would do most of her packing this weekend and finish up the last odds and ends after work on Friday. She would take a cab to the airport, check her luggage, eat supper at one of the restaurants, and then catch her flight. Her mind was in turmoil. Does she tell Joel? Does she tell anyone where she's going? She rubbed the back of her neck with her right hand and sat back. "How foolish," she giggled. "Joel's father owns the company, so within minutes it will be known that Margaret has requested vacation time."

First thing Monday morning, Margaret procured the time off from work. She sat back in her Perot Genuine leather chair and giggled. "I'm sure Joel will hear that I've just taken three weeks off from work."

At that moment Joel came to her office and gazed at her. "I was just told that you're taking three weeks out of work. Why didn't you mention it to Titus and me on Friday? How come you never said anything to me when I called on Saturday and Sunday?" He gestured with his right hand. "Are you going away?"

She nodded her head. "I did a lot of soul searching over the weekend, I do believe you and Titus are right that I need to take time and mourn. Perhaps a different scenery will help me to not always see my mother." She bit her bottom lip. "I've been sitting in her chair, sleeping in her bed, and I believe I need to get away." She gestured with her right hand. "So, I'm going to a chateau in the French Alps for a couple of weeks."

"What chateau?"

"It's called the Chateau de Paix, and it seems like it's ideal for peace and tranquility."

Joel scratched the back of his head with his right hand. "I've heard about that place from someone. It's seems last year three women disappeared after being there."

Margaret giggled. "Rumors seem to grow like plants on a rock and spread up overnight with little foundation." She gestured with her right hand. "I mean, really, Joel. If the chateau was suspected of such a bizarre happening, wouldn't the authorities know? I mean, the chateau has been cleared. All three women caught their flights home, picked up their luggage at the terminal, and then disappeared."

"I understand, but it does seem quite bazaar they can't find any trail of the women after they picked up their luggage at the airport."

"It never ceases to amaze me what people will believe." Margaret said, rubbing the back of her neck with her right hand. "I talked to the woman who owns it, and she was extremely sweet. I told her I needed to get away from the daily stress of things, and that I lost my mother last month." She picked up the brochure. "I explained that I'm an avid bird watcher and have taken thousands of photos." She handed him the brochure. "The woman said I was making a wise decision to come there. It's secluded in the French Alps, beautiful surroundings, and many species of birds." She giggled. "That why it's called the Chateau of Peace."

Joel read the brochure. "It does sound like it will afford you some peace and tranquility." He cupped her right hand with both of his hands. "Please use it as a time to allow the Lord to comfort and heal you. Remember there is the light at the end of the tunnel." He gave her a kiss. "I'll get back to work. If you need my help for anything, please let me know." He paused. "When do you leave?"

"Late Friday night. I couldn't book it before early evening on the fifth which is Saturday. This way I'll have time to make sure I have everything needed." She paused. "I'll be taking a cab to the airport due to the lateness of the hour. I'll be coming back about eight in the evening on Sunday the twentieth."

Joel's eyebrows squished together. "Certainly, I can pick you up then." He gestured with his right hand. "It's going to be a rough two weeks without seeing you." He scratched the back of his head with his right hand. "Blessed are they that mourn: for they shall be comforted." He placed his right hand on her right hand. "You need to take time to mourn in order to be healed. All I care about is you getting the peace you so need." He laughed. "When you get back we have to discuss something very important."

"Can't we discuss it now? I mean, if it's important, it shouldn't wait."

"I just think you'll be more able to concentrate on our discussion if you've had time to grieve the loss of your mother." He gestured with both hands. "I don't mean you'll be all healed. That will take time. I just mean if you can get an understanding from the Lord why she wasn't healed when you prayed." He paused. "We can pray for something. But if it's not his will, we must trust in his love for us. He is omniscient and knows what he's planned for each one of us." His eyebrows squished together. "I recently read a book that will help anyone who desires to understand God's love. It's described in chapter three where the author reveals the love of God through the coverings of the tabernacle." He gestured with his right hand. "I have it in my office, if you're interested?"

"I think it might be helpful." She said, sighing. "What's the name of it?"

"It's called *Storms Are Faith's Workout: Preparing Christians for Spiritual Ambush* by R. C. Jette."

"Well, did the author know about my storm?" She said, giggling.

He put up his right forefinger. "Give me a minute, and I'll get it."

Chapter Three

The Gaunt Man

WORKS' PRESSURE WAS LIKE a millstone grinding Margaret down little by little. When Friday evening finally came, she was a basket case riding to the airport. It seemed like a storm was still raging within and without. It was not enough that she saw Carlotta pass Joel another note, but his being so aloof about what he wanted to discuss with her, had her convinced he's going to call off the engagement.

She hurried into the terminal and found it as busy as usual. All the scurrying and the restlessness of people had her nerves on edge. In her anxiety, she ate about a half dozen candy bars, downed several bags of chips, and several diet cokes. She ended up forgoing supper after all the indulgence of junk food. The queasiness in her stomach left her unsure if she was well or not.

When Margaret finally boarded the plane, she was pleased to have a seat to herself. As she took her seat, she tried to take some deep breaths and put Joel and Carlotta out of her mind. After an hour in the air, calmness began to integrate into her being, and her taut nerves began to ease into serenity.

She placed her long black hair behind her ears with both hands. "This is exactly what I needed," she whispered. "A time to sit on the sidelines and get out of the rat race." She sat back, closed her eyes, and sighed. "My next two weeks will be eating, sleeping, bird-watching, hiking, more eating, and sleeping. No time schedule, no rat-race, no diet, and no one to answer to. What blissful tranquility." She smiled. "It surely will be the chateau of peace."

From the airport, a limousine would be waiting to take her to a large hotel in the town nearest the chateau. Once there, someone from the chateau would pick her up and take her to the hide-a-way. To avoid confusion, she was to wear a red name tag and stand outside the main lobby.

While she waited, she felt like a child about to visit an amusement park. Elation surged through every fiber of her being. She was in France at last. Anxious for her ride, she turned to check the time. From behind, a boney hand touched her shoulder, she let out a scream as a spasm ran through her body, and turned around to see who the hand belonged to.

"Margaret Anderson," said a gaunt man whose face closed as if guarding a secret.

With staggered breaths, she reached out with her right hand to shake a bony white glove.

"I'm to bring you to the chateau," he said, clenching his jaw.

Margaret felt a chill run down her spine. A long nose and cold predatory eyes seemed to compound his disagreeable visage.

"Is this all your luggage?" He said, picking up her things and walking away.

"I believe that's all I'll need for two weeks." She said, practically tripping over her feet to catch up.

Once outside, he put her suitcases into the trunk of a black limousine, opened the door, and beckoned her to get in. As she stepped into the vehicle, she managed to utter a monosyllable. "Thanks."

As Margaret rode towards the chateau, she became absorbed with the magic of the place. If she had ever envisioned "Paradise," it would have been like this. She heard birds singing an unknown lullaby, flowers dramatized the tune, and a soft breeze flowed through the open windows like an incantation that bid her to rest.

She sat back, closed her eyes, and relished in the overwhelming sense of well-being. Her mind questioned why she had never found this place before. Would this be the means of healing the loss of her mother? Was Joel really going to break off the engagement? Is there a romantic relationship between him and Carlotta? She gave a heavy sigh and tried to calm her inner restlessness. The whole purpose for this trip was to unwind and receive healing for the loss of her mother, and not be overwhelmed with everything that's going on.

When Margaret opened her eyes, she noticed the driver staring at her in the review mirror, her stomach knotted as a sense of fear lay ready to emerge. His beady eyes made her feel like she was lusted and hated in one emotion. An incredible sense of alarm tried to strangle her emotions. She felt guilty that his appearance upset her and forced a smile. But she could have sworn that his eyes narrowed with disgust before he quickly looked away.

Margaret felt absurd that she allowed such bizarre fancies to overwhelm her. She determined to quit allowing her feelings to get the better of her. Besides, how can the man hate someone he has just met? She pulled herself together and leaned forward. "Excuse me. I don't believe I got your name."

"Blagdon Fowler," he said, watching her through the rear-view mirror.

Her skin crawled, but she was adamant to control her emotions. After all, he couldn't help his emaciated visage was so unattractive. Perhaps, he found her attractive. She could not count the times people had commented that her beautiful blue eyes were stunning. Besides, she was there to relax and sort things out, not to be judging someone's appearance.

Margaret decided to carry on a conversation with him and break the ice. "Are there many guests at the chateau?" She said, trying to sound friendly.

"Two besides you."

"Will more be coming?"

"A crowd would hardly make the next two weeks a hide-a-way," he sneered. "The brochure made it quite clear that this is a time to get away from the hustle and bustle of life and experience peace and tranquility."

Margaret nodded in agreement, and sat back. But his reaction confused her. Her mind whirled with questions. Why only three? Joel said three women disappeared last year after visiting the chateau. Is she ignoring the signs? But the authorities cleared the chateau. It was a known fact the women left the chateau, caught their flight home, picked up their luggage, and then disappeared. Are all these questions and negative feelings the result of my reading gothic mysteries? A few have warned of their unhealthy consequences at such a time as this.

She shook her head at the absurdity of it all. As if she couldn't separate fantasy from reality. Pulling the book that Joel had given her to read out of her purse, the front and back cover convinced her that she needed to learn how to overcome her storm. Did she really understand God's love? Did she understand God at all? She was raised to believe that God loves her. How could a God who loves not heal her mother?

Margaret knew her faith was under attack, and she's been unable to rise above it. Her heart cried out for God to enable her to be standing when this storm is over. She rubbed the back of her neck with her right hand and tried to silence the questions. She determined to read the book as soon as possible. If it would aid her in gaining an understanding that would encourage some much needed healing, she welcomed its help.

After all, the whole purpose of this vacation was to experience peace and quiet, while receiving healing for her grief. Only solitude from the stress and busyness of her daily life would enable her sorrow to mend.

Her mind went to the others and questioned if they desired solitude or would they be pests. She smiled as she saw the foolishness in her thoughts. After all, why else would they be there. The brochure was quite clear it was a time to get away from the stress of daily life and unwind. She resolved to take advantage of this time.

Chapter Four

The Chateau

MARGARET DECIDED TO SIT back and take in the beauty of the scenery all around. Again, she listened to the melodious songs of the birds, how the flowers seemed to dance to the tune, and the calmness the soft breeze created. She felt such elation and joy nourishing her. Finally, she would be able to allow herself to confront her mother's death.

As she enjoyed the sense of peace that encouraged her, her eyes caught sight of this magnificent edifice that practically caused her to jump out of her seat. "Wow!" She said. "Is that the chateau?"

Nodding his head like he hears it all the time, Blagdon smirked at her amazement. But Margaret could not believe her eyes. Before her stood this edifice that resembled a medieval castle from the pages of a gothic thriller. Suddenly fear flashed the castle of Udolpho through her mind, but she was resolute to overcome all nonsense and enjoy the magnificence of the place.

When they pulled up to the chateau, Margaret expected a multitude of servants to greet her. Instead there was a man who looked about forty with greying temples and deep-blue eyes that seemed to beg rescue from unseen shackles, and an attractive olive complexioned woman wearing a red dress who reached to shake her hand. "Margaret Anderson, welcome to my chateau. My name is Brenna Martinez."

Margaret shook her hand and said, "It's my pleasure. I can't convey how I've looked forward to being here."

Brenna touched the middle-aged man's arm. "This is my husband Claudio." Then her eyes seemed to narrow as she gestured towards Blagdon. "You've met my twin brother."

Margaret forced a smile. "Yes, he was most helpful with some questions I had on the way here." As they headed towards the entrance of the chateau, her mind was in a whirlwind. How can he be her twin brother? You could have fooled me. She is absolutely stunning, and he is undeniably homely. Then again people don't choose their family. Maybe once you could ignore his looks, he was a nice guy. She shook her head. What did she care? At present, her own problems are enough. Her mind had no more room for muddle.

Margaret's eyes began to take in the chateau. How long she glared spellbound at the gatehouse flanked by huge towers, she didn't know. But when she sensed their fixed stares, she nearly fell up the steps. "Glad to meet all of you. I mean, thanks for having me." She gazed down at the stairs and tried to compose herself. Why had she thanked them for having her? She was paying dearly for this vacation. She blinked her eyes and focused on getting past the awe of the place and start vacationing. Yet, she could not shake off the inner sense of foreboding.

Confusion seemed to cause her to be unsettled, as she followed them into the chateau which was like a medieval castle. She looked with wonder at the extent and grandeur of the great hall. To the right was a marble stair-case that reminded her of some nobleman and noblewoman stepping down to welcome their guests to dinner.

Margaret was somewhat dazed at its splendor as she was introduced to the other guests. Isabelle Lefebvre-Duval, a green-eyed blond sat with her arms folded as if angry at the world. When introduced, she gave a chilled nod. Abigail Simpson, an attractive African-American woman, rushed to welcome her with a cheery smile. What a contrast to Isabelle. However, Margaret wasn't concerned about making friends or getting involved with anyone's plagues. She had enough troubles of her own. Solitude was the only companion she welcomed for this vacation.

Brenna pointed to a chair and had Margaret sit. "I'll be out with supper in a few minutes. I was waiting for Margaret to arrive." She clasped her hands. "Now that you're all here, I can proceed."

Margaret was famished and determined to stuff herself, and she didn't care what anyone thought. Her stomach growled as she caught the aroma of baked ham, scalloped potatoes, and green bean casserole.

All night Margaret was haunted with nightmares of the chateau hiding dark secrets. When she could focus her thoughts, she realized she must have drunk too much wine at supper. However, she didn't remember drinking any wine, but she seemed to be in a whirlwind of emotions.

The morning sunlight brought the fragrance of freshly brewed coffee to her room and renewed her spirits. She hurriedly took a shower, dressed, and grabbed what she would need to go bird-watching.

As she entered the room, Brenna seemed to be disturbed. "Well, sleeping beauty is finally up."

Margaret felt her face blush. "I didn't rest well, strange bed." She took a seat. "I'm sure I'll get used to it."

Brenna nodded her head. "Yes, it is sometimes difficult sleeping in a strange bed." She immediately piled Margaret's plate with ham, scrambled eggs, and home fries. "I know you have an appetite, so I was ready for you this morning."

"I decided to forget my diet while on vacation," Margaret said, clearing her throat.

"If you don't mind me saying, you could use a few extra pounds." She gestured with her right hand. "I mean, you are rather thin." Her eyebrows raised. "You're not anorexic or something are you?"

"I don't think so. I mean, I don't look to vomit after I eat. It's something I started to do after my mother's death." She sighed. "You see my fiancé, all of a sudden, started to pass notes to a girl at work who looks like an Italian model." She buttered a roll. "As a matter of fact, you look like you could be one yourself. However, you are more stunning than Carlotta."

Brenna's eyes blinked and her head shook. "You're just trying to be friendly."

"Believe me, I don't say anything to flatter if it's not true." Her face screwed up. "Where's Isabelle and Abigail?"

"They were up at the crack of dawn," she said, filling Margaret's coffee cup.

"I guess my idea of a vacation includes rest," Margaret said, feeling her face blush. "I can understand Claudio and Blagdon, but I thought Isabelle and Abigail were on vacation."

"Abigail was up before anyone. She was anxious to take the canoe down river. Isabelle seemed to be in a hurry to just get out in nature for the peace."

After breakfast, Margaret grabbed her camera and notebook. She was determined to do some serious bird watching. If luck was on her side, she'd get some pictures of rare species.

She found herself in the woods between the grassy knolls of the mountain filled with plants and wildflowers resembling a color wheel of vibrant colors of red, blue, purple, green, orange, and yellow. Overwhelmed by the wonder of the scene, she hadn't noticed someone was watching her.

"How's your bird watching coming?" Claudio said.

At the sound of his voice, Margaret almost tripped over her own feet. "I . . . I haven't done much yet." She caught her breath. "Nice day," she said, smiling. "I was enthralled in the splendor of the place. It's like another world."

"Yes, the glory of the place does seem to hypnotize one."

"I just want to take advantage of its wonder. Have no idea when I'll get away again."

He hung his head and kicked the shrub at his feet. "Vacations don't come often."

Margaret was touched with the thought the hosts of a resort might need a vacation. "I guess it is difficult to get away when there's only three of you running this place. How do you do it?"

"No, no, no," He said wiping his face with a rag. "We just started this last year for the two-week getaway. All the rest of the year, we have a full staff inside and outside." He gestured with his right hand. "There's grounds men, maids, launderers, cooks, maintenance workers, and what all." He gave a chuckle and shook his head. "We couldn't keep this place up ourselves."

Margaret felt heat stealing into her face. "I should've guessed as much. But where are they?"

"Brenna gives the staff the two weeks off every year and a bonus so they can vacation wherever they want. That's why she decided to have this two-week getaway for three guests needing the peace and solitude the chateau affords."

"Brenna welcomed me to her chateau, but isn't it Blagdon's also?"

"Oh no, her grandmother left it entirely to Brenna."

"Is that why Blagdon seems to unhappy?"

Claudio rubbed his forehead as if contemplating his thoughts and stared at the ground. "It's not that. He was supposed to get married about three years ago, but she didn't show up for the wedding." He sighed. "It seems she believed he was owner or half owner of the chateau. She nonchalantly asked the night before the wedding. Anyway, discovering he had no part of it, she took off and left him standing at the church."

"Oh my! How horrible." She paused. "I am so sorry for him."

He rubbed his right arm with his left hand. "I thought they might be reconciling last year." He gestured with both hands. "Janet was one of the women staying here for the two-week peace and solitude." His eyebrows squished together. "I was surprised when she showed up, but Brenna said all was fine." He looked down at his feet. "Anyway, he hasn't been the same since she disappeared. He's lost so much weight." He paused. "Well," he said, shrugging his shoulders, "I had better get this wood back. Besides," he said, raising his voice an octave, "you're on vacation."

Margaret nodded. Her mind raced. Hearing about someone being rejected touched too close to home. She didn't want to deal with Joel until her mind could rationalize. She really needed to get on with her bird watching.

Dusk fell before Margaret realized it. She was pleased with the results of the day. She had a great picture of a golden eagle with a wing span of at least seven feet. She had a recording of a black grouse singing a loud, bubbling, and somewhat dove-like song. She had gotten a picture of an alpine wallcreeper with its blue grey plumage and its extraordinary crimson wings. Her favorite was a male eagle owl about twenty-five inches long with its erect ear tuffs and orange eyes.

As she looked around her surroundings, she was enthralled by the sounds of the wind whistling along the slopes and the rustling of the trees. The fragrance of pine needles and the crisp air made her feel like she was in paradise.

Suddenly, she came back to reality. "I've got to get back to the chateau." As she hurried back, branches snapped and crunched under her feet. Although somewhat disoriented, she managed to find her way back. On her way in, Blagdon flashed her a look of disdain. "About time, isn't it?" His vexation was evident as he stood with hands on his hips. "Brenna's kept dinner for you. You could be more considerate of other people."

She remembered what Claudio had told her, and foraged for an excuse. "I am so sorry. I forgot my watch."

"Humph!" He scowled and walked off.

As Margaret watched him huff away, she wished she'd thought to compliment him somehow. She decided to do it tomorrow.

Her growling stomach took over her senses. She followed the scent into the great hall and found it empty except for Brenna. She took a seat and thought how there's an advantage to being late. She would eat alone. After last night, her meal would be more satisfying without Isabelle's cold stares.

All her concerns vanished at the sight of roast beef, all the fixings, and plum pudding for desert. Feasting like a pig, she felt no guilt. Her diet could proceed after vacation. Too stuffed to move, she was dazzled at the arms and the armor adorning the massive walls. Huge flails, battle-axes, daggers, swords, several cone-shaped helmets, and chain mail hung wherever there wasn't a tapestry. Her face screwed up at the odd statues in each corner on a pedestal. Why hadn't she noticed them before?

Chapter Five

New Friends

MARGARET NOTICED BRENNA WATCHING her. "Those statues are somewhat strange for the rest of the décor," she said, her eyebrows squishing together. "They are rather strange with multiple heads and hands, blue bodies, blue face and throat." Her eyes widened. "What are they? Do they represent something?"

"My grandmother was Hindu and had her favorite gods. If I was to inherit, I had to promise to leave them. My grandmother was adamant that they were to stay intact." She gave a heavy sigh. "I will not go back on my promise to her. However, I wish they weren't here." She gestured to each god. "That one with four heads and four arms is Brahma. The blue one with four hands is Vishnu. Shiva is the one with a human body, blue face, and a blue throat. Durga is the one riding the lion with multiple hands; she was my grandmother's favorite." She paused. "As a matter of fact, there are large replicas in the medieval garden that you may experience alone. I have a notepad at the door leading out to the garden. You just sign your name for the night you desire to spend time alone in there."

Margaret's eyes widened. "Did you say a medieval garden?"

Brenna chuckled. "Yes. It's full of ripe fruit, vegetables, and herbs at this time of year." She gestured towards the table. "If you're finished, I'll clean up."

"No. I mean, I'm finished, but let me help you clean up. My mother and I always cleaned up together." Her eyes teared. "It's so difficult without her. I lost my father when I was two, so I don't remember him." She giggled. "Anyway, let me help you clean up."

"But you're on vacation."

"I know. But how many times will I have the pleasure of cleaning up inside an edifice such as this?" Margaret said, giggling.

Margaret finished helping Brenna. But on her way to her room, she questioned why the place seemed to haunt and hypnotize at the same time. The foreboding caused her insides to quiver. Entering her room, she gave a heavy sigh. "It has to be how strung out I've been since my mother's illness and death. Perhaps, I shouldn't have been reading *The Mysteries of Udolpho* at this time." She sat on her bed. "I'm acting like Emily at Udolpho, but there's no Montoni here. Claudio is a sweetheart. I really like Brenna. Blagdon, on the other hand, is weird. Yet, when you've suffered from love's rejection, it can do a number on the most agreeable person."

She tossed for hours trying to figure out what to do when she returned home. Should she cancel the wedding? Should she make the first move? Was she having a nervous collapse? She did see them passing notes. She wasn't imagining that, for Titus saw it too.

Margaret got up. "Perhaps, I need to read chapter three of the book Joel gave me." After she finished the chapter, she laid down. "Lord, I never knew how special I am to you. I'm your priceless jewel." She said, tears rolling down her face. "Lord, I don't understand why you took my mother, but I do know you love me more than I ever realized." She sat up, crying. "How many Christians never get past the first covering? No wonder Joel told me to read that book."

Morning came too swiftly, but the merry chirping of birds beckoned Margaret to get up. Stretching, she walked over to the window, opened it, and inhaled the fresh air. As she looked out, she realized her window overlooked the medieval garden. "Oh my! It's majestic. I really must sit in that garden. I believe I'll sign the notepad today."

She dressed and hurried down for breakfast. Her stomach growled as she entered the hall. She stopped as she eyed the table. Again, there was no one there.

"Well, I see sleeping beauty is finally here," Brenna said, chuckling.

"What time do you start serving breakfast? I honestly thought I was early enough today."

"I start serving at six. It's now half past eight." She gestured to a chair. "Abigail and Isabelle are sitting here waiting for me to serve. They are quite anxious about getting outside."

"Sorry. I will be here earlier tomorrow morning."

Brenna poured Margaret's coffee. "It's okay. After all, they were in bed when you were helping me clean up last night."

"Thank you." She buttered an English muffin. "If you don't mind, I'd really like to help clean up after breakfast." She shrugged her shoulders. "You do so much. I mean, packing us such a lunch so we don't have to come back until supper." Margaret paused. "After I do my bird watching today, I'd like to take the canoe down the river in the moonlight. Could I miss supper tonight? Of course, when I get back, I'll help you clean up."

Brenna's face screwed up. "Of course, you may." She shook her head. "I'll not have you going to bed hungry; I'll keep supper aside for you." She gestured towards Margaret with her right hand. "I mean, if you miss too many meals, you might just fade away. You really do need to put on a few pounds."

"Okay. I promise to eat more if you'll let me help you clean up." She put out her right hand. "Is it a deal?"

"Seeing you enjoy it so much, I'll keep that until you come," Brenna said, shaking Margaret's hand.

"Oh yes, I do believe that I would like to have a night in the garden." She gestured with both hands. "Not tonight, though."

"Abigail has it booked for tonight, but it's open tomorrow night." Brenna refilled Margaret's coffee cup. "I'll put your name in while you finish eating."

Margaret finished the clean-up with Brenna and headed out to enjoy the solitude of the scenery and bird watching. She found herself skipping down a path. How wonderful it was to be here. She felt an adrenaline rush at the thought of taking the canoe down the river in the moonlight. She had been waiting for the full moon.

As she skipped along, she was looking up at the tree tops. Suddenly she tumbled over something in the path. She heard a scream as she fell forward. A hand helped her up. "Are you okay?"

Margaret looked into the green eyes of Isabelle. "I think so."

"I dropped my backpack and was picking it up, or I would have seen you coming." Isabelle said, her voice weakening. "I am so sorry." She paused. "Are you sure you're okay?"

"An angel must have cushioned my fall."

Isabelle bit her bottom lip. "Are you a Christian?"

"Yes. But since my mother died last month, I don't think I've been acting like one."

Isabelle looked down at her feet. "I guess I haven't been acting much like one either."

Margaret giggled. "I must admit your cold stares were quite unsettling." She brushed off debris from her fall. "It was difficult eating with such bitterness being directed at me."

"It's just that you remind of the woman my husband divorced me for. I do believe you would pass for her sister." Her eyes teared. "I never saw it coming. He didn't want me to work after we were married, so I was the dutiful housewife. Yet, George left me for a woman who was vice-president of his company. He claimed they had more in common." She wiped her eyes. "I could've been vice-president if he'd let me work."

"I'm so sorry." She glared into Isabelle's eyes. "It's so strange how you always think you're the only one going through something." She sat on a log. "I'm here to get over the death of my mother and the fact I believe my fiancé is about to call off the wedding. He's been passing notes back and forth with the CEO secretary." She took a drink of water. "As a matter of fact, If I didn't know otherwise, I'd be convinced you're Carlotta's sister."

"What did you say?"

"If I didn't know otherwise, I'd believe you're Carlotta's sister."

"You wouldn't happen to mean Carlotta De Luca, would you?"

"Yes, that's her name. Do you know her?"

"We went to college together, and everyone thought we were sisters. After college, she went back to Italy, I married George. Somehow, we lost touch." She sat on a log next to Margaret. "I find it really difficult to believe that Carlotta would be up to something like that. I mean, a friend of ours at college was engaged to this guy. But when he met Carlotta, he was making passes at her. Let me tell you, she flat out rebuked him." She exhaled, heavily. "I'm so sorry for the way I've treated you. I thought I was pretty much healed until I saw you." She gestured with both hands. "George's infidelity came rushing back like a locomotive. I really thought I'd forgiven him."

"Forgiveness seems to be a problem with many Christians," Margaret's said, her face flushing. "I think I have been holding something against the Lord for not healing my mother." She paused. "I'm so sorry, I interrupted you." She gestured with her right hand. "Please continue."

Isabelle gazed into Margaret's blue eyes. "This is most unsettling. I mean, the Lord only forgives us as we forgive others." Isabelle bit her bottom lip. "Meeting you revealed that I was holding onto unforgiveness. Once the Lord helped me understand why George left, I was humbled. But I didn't realize I hadn't forgiven him." She bit her bottom lip. "I guess I was still angry. I have a degree in business administration, and George said I'd be an asset once he took over his grandfather's business after he graduated. However, after we were married, he said he didn't want to come home to no supper, chores to do, etc. Anyway, he wanted me to be a housewife, and I submitted to his will. After five years of marriage, he leaves me for the vice president of his company claiming he had more in common with her." She reached into her backpack and pulled out a book. "This book is what helped me after George's infidelity." Her face screwed up. "The strangest thing is that after he left, I was angry for giving five years of my life. I even questioned if I ever loved him or loved the fact I was married."

"Wow!" Margaret reached into her backpack and pulled out her book. "My fiancé gave me this and said it would help me understand God's love."

"It wasn't that I doubted God's love. I couldn't understand why when I'd been so faithful to him, my husband would leave me." Isabelle opened her book and flipped the pages. "It was in chapter five that's entitled, *Storms Appear Without An Alarm*. In it is revealed that Job's storms are the epitome of what an ambush is. He had no idea that good people could be overtaken by such adversity." She exhaled, heavily. "Job was ambushed by Satan with utter malice because he was pleasing to God." Her hands trembled. "I was pleasing to God and that's why the devil attacked me."

Margaret hugged her. "I had no idea of that. I mean, I'm flabbergasted. I really do have to finish reading this book." She placed her long black hair behind her ears with both hands. "I truly sense that it will all turn out for your good." She giggled. "That's what I keep being told, but I truly believe it for you." Her blue eyes widened. "What a vacation this is turning into. I should call it a spiritual healing hospital." She giggled. "I can't thank the Lord enough for having Joel give me that book."

They both laughed.

"It was my pastor that suggested I read it." Isabelle put her copy of *Storms Are Faith's Workout* back into her backpack. "Perhaps, we can talk about it more at supper."

"I won't be there for supper. It's a full moon, and I've been wanting to take a canoe down the river in the moonlight." She giggled. "But I am determined to be earlier for breakfast."

"Well, tomorrow at breakfast, then." Isabelle put her backpack on. "I do thank God I'm not superstitious. All those Hindu gods could be quite unsettling."

"Did Brenna tell you about them?"

"No, there were a couple of sisters from India who were in my classes at college. They each carried miniature replicas of Vishnu, the preserver, and Shiva, the destroyer."

"I've never seen any of them until here in the Great Hall. Brenna said her grandmother was Hindu and her favorite was Durga." She rubbed the back of her neck with her right hand. "It's so strange how people can believe in gods that are created by human hands. My God is so powerful that he holds all the waters of the earth in the palm of his hand."

"Amen!" Isabelle said, taking Margaret's right hand into hers. "Lord, thank you for my new friend. Help us to allow you to heal us, trust in your love for us, and know that whether or not we understand, you are working all this out for our good because we love you."

They both said, "Amen!"

Chapter Six

Confession Is Good for the Soul

AFTER ISABELLE WALKED AWAY, Margaret noticed Claudio watching from behind a tree. She didn't know whether to pretend not to see him or wave. She decided to wave.

As he walked towards her, his shoulders slumped. "I didn't mean to listen in on your conversation, but I was coming from my sanctuary of solitude. I try to go there every day to think." He ran the fingers of his right hand through his brown curls. "It's strange how I just thought the people that come here are frivolous with mediocre problems." His face flushed. "I believed I'm the only one suffering."

Margaret's blue eyes widened. "You live in this beautiful place and your wife is stunning." She placed her hair behind her ears with both hands. "It's like paradise here. I've never felt so peaceful."

He kicked a twig with his right foot. "Yes, but when God put them out of paradise, everything became thorns and thistles." He rubbed his right arm with his left hand. "It's no longer tiptoeing through the tulips, but being pricked and bleeding daily."

Margaret sat back down on her log. "I guess you have me confused."

"After hearing you and Isabelle confess to each other, I think confession is good for the soul." He paused. "I believe it's time for me to get some healing." He sat on a log next to Margaret. "When I met Brenna, I fell head over heels in love with her. Her beauty hypnotized me." He grabbed his head with both hands. "You see, my parents own a magnificent ski resort in the Swiss Alps and the Villa Hermosa in Argentina." He looked down at his feet. "They didn't want me to marry Brenna. Even my pastor tried to help me see it would be a mistake." His deep-blue eyes watered. "But when you're blind and deceived, no one can reason with you." He threw up both hands. "God knows they tried, but their words fell on deaf ears." He paused. "I wonder how many times Christians refuse to hear truth because they are bent on having their will and not God's?"

Margaret's mind raced trying to find a response. "Blind and deceived?"

"I came here for a vacation to see the difference between our resort and this famous chateau. Immediately, Brenna set her cap on me. Of course, I was smitten. Anyway, I thought she loved me, but she loved the idea of owning a chateau in France, a ski resort in Switzerland, and a villa in Argentina." He wiped his eyes with his handkerchief. "My parents saw through her. After I married her, they disinherited me. I've not heard from them in five years. Now, Brenna treats me like one of the servants and reminds me how much I owe her for being here."

"Why are you staying married to someone who doesn't love you? I mean, if you divorced her, you and your parents could be reconciled."

"They don't accept divorce because of unhappiness." He sighed, heavily. "It would have to be something really dreadful that she did for them to accept divorce." He stood up. "I am sorry for unloading on you. After all, you've recently lost your mother and are dealing with a possible wedding cancelation."

"This is so bazaar," Margaret said, giggling. "I find out Isabelle is trying to get over her husband divorcing her." She gestured towards him with her right hand. "I thought you looked unhappy the first day we met, but I had no idea it was so sad."

He ran the fingers of his right hand through his brown curls. "May I see that book you both mentioned?"

"Of course," Margaret said, pulling it out of her backpack. "You can take it now, I've got a day of bird watching and canoeing down the river in the moonlight ahead of me. I'll not be reading any more today."

He took it into his hands. "*Storms Are Faith's Workout: Preparing Christians for Spiritual Ambition,*" he said, turning it over to see the back cover. "Wow! It's talking to me. I am surely struggling with the storms of this life and feel overwhelmed with the constant onslaught." He put it inside his knapsack. "I've caught up with whatever Brenna wanted me to do this morning." He laughed. "I hurried so I could get to my place of solitude." He gestured with his right hand. "Time to head back to my place of solitude and read." His face drained of color. "Don't let Brenna know you and I were talking. And whatever you do don't mention this book to me. What I'll do is while she is busy tonight, I'll slip it under your bedroom door." His face lit up. "Let me show you my place of solitude. I have a metal box that I keep some things in. It would be too much to carry it all each day. You can leave the book in there each morning, and I'll return it under your bedroom door each night." He paused. "When I've finished reading, I'll just put a paper clip on the front cover so you don't have to put it there each morning."

As they walked, Claudio seemed to be contemplating something. "Isabelle seems like a devoted Christian." He gestured with his right hand. "As I listened to her speak, she sounded like a woman of God."

"I believe she is. That's why she was troubled as to why God allowed her husband to divorce her."

"God can't stop us from doing what we have made up our minds to do. I certainly know that. He gave us a free will, and he won't interfere with it." He sighed, heavily. "You have no idea how many times I wish he would. But like my pastor taught, God wants us to choose to love and serve him. He'll have no puppets who are forced to do what string is pulled."

"My mother taught that also." Margaret's eyes filled with tears. "I prayed for God to heal her and he didn't." She turned to look at him. "First Peter chapter two says *by whose stripes ye were healed.*

31

My mother was healed on Calvary, yet she died at forty-nine." She bit her bottom lip. "Plus, God took my father when I was only two. I don't remember him."

Claudio looked down at the ground. "I am so sorry. How did they die?"

"My father died as a test pilot for the United States Air Force and my mother died of cancer."

"That's sad," he said, his voice trembling. "I'm the one, through disobeying the will of God, who has been without my parents for five years." He looked down at his feet. "I sorely miss them."

"Have you tried to call them and say so?"

"After their letter disinheriting me, I've not been able to contact them." He paused. "I guess, I was afraid they wouldn't speak to me."

Once again, Margaret got caught up in her surroundings. The soft breeze brought the sweet scent of the pine trees like freshly mowed grass, and her feet crunched the spongy layers of dead pine needles and twigs underfoot.

Suddenly, Claudio put his arm out to stop her. "Let me move all this debris," he said, laughing. "It's my wall of protection to keep any one from finding my place of solitude." He cleared it away and had her stand out of the way until he covered it back up. "Now, it's a little tricky for a bit, but it's well worth it."

Margaret followed carefully behind. "This is like something out of a suspense novel."

He nodded his head. "We're almost there." He stopped and pointed to his right.

"Wow! It's like a little island. How enchanting with the babbling brook or spring flowing all around it." Her blue eyes widened. "How did you ever find it?"

"About three years ago, I was so unhappy, I just found myself walking blindly through the woods when I stumbled upon this place. I do mean stumbled," he said, laughing. "I was walking aimlessly and tripped over a log. When I stood up, I saw this place.

After that, I used wood and brush to hide it. I have the pile on the outside for when I leave, and I have the pile on the inside to cover when I enter through the opening." He helped her over the stream that ran through the area. "Here's the box." He sat down and chuckled. "How will you ever get back here? I don't think this is a good plan." He ran the fingers of his right hand through his curly hair. "I think it would be better for me to meet you where we were today. I'll stay hidden and make sure no one sees me and then you can give me the book." He rubbed his right arm with his left hand. "Then I'll slip it back under your door at night."

Margaret giggled. "I have a better idea. Why don't you just finish reading it, and then you can slip it under my bedroom door after."

He sat down on a chair made out of a log. "I do believe that's a winner." His eyes took on a haunted look. "Here I am sitting on a log when I have an MBA in business administration and a law degree. My parents wanted me to take over the business in Switzerland and they were going to spend their retirement years at their villa in Argentina." He gestured with both hands. "My parents are faithful to the Lord, so I believe he will turn things around for their sake."

"I believe that also. We may miss the mark at times. But when we repent of the sin, he is so loving and merciful." She bit her bottom lip. "I never understood how much he loved me until I read it in that book. What a revelation."

"Well, I do believe I feel lighter." Claudio chuckled. "Confession is good for the soul." He stood up. "I think it's time for you to enjoy your vacation."

"That's an excellent idea. However, you will have to show me how to get out of here," Margaret said, giggling.

Chapter Seven

Moonlight and Mystery

MARGARET FOUND HERSELF ENGULFED in the grandeur of the forest. The tall trees seemed to rise up out of the earth to brush the sky. The sun shone through the tree tops creating a mystical glow on the carpet of wildflowers.

"Let the heavens rejoice, and let the earth be glad; let the sea roar, and the fulness thereof. Let the field be joyful, and all that is therein: then shall all the trees of the wood rejoice." Margaret said, her eyes filling with tears. "Oh, Lord, thank you for bringing me here. I'd forgotten how to enjoy your beautiful creation."

"His creation is truly beautiful."

Margaret screeched at the voice behind her. As she turned, Abigail's eyes bulged. "I didn't mean to frighten you." She grabbed Margaret's right hand. "I am truly sorry."

"I'm fine," Margaret said, breathing heavily. "I was lost in the majesty of God's creation, and I didn't hear you coming." She sat on a fallen tree. "Are you a Christian?"

"Yes. I've been born again since I was ten. That's twenty-three years ago." Her brown eyes filled with tears. "I fell in love with this doctor who I met while finishing my residency at Rockdale Hospital. He's African-American like me, claimed to love the Lord, and we seemed to have so much in common." She sat next to Margaret. "However, he kept pressuring me to." She paused. "You know what I mean." She rubbed her temples with the fingers of both hands.

"I told him I believed the word of God that says no fornicator will inherit the kingdom of God. He claimed that was before, but once Jesus died on the cross, all our sins are forgiven."

"What!"

Abigail leaned forward. "I know! He believes you can say the sinner's prayer and live like the devil and go to heaven." She gestured with both hands. "There will be no devils in heaven nor will there be any who have lived like one. We are to be holy as God is holy."

"Lest there be any fornicator, or profane person, as Esau, who for one morsel of meat sold his birthright." She paused. "In other words, for the lust of his flesh, Esau sold his birthright. We can't lose our salvation or birthright, but we can sell it to satisfy our fleshly appetites." Margaret placed her long black hair behind her ears with both hands. "Once you sell something, you no longer have it." Her blue eyes widened. "It's gone. In the case of our salvation, we never paid for it. Jesus gave it to us freely upon repenting of our sins and accepting his plan of salvation. So, if we sell it like Esau to satisfy our fleshly lusts, it can't be bought back. We will die in our trespasses and sins." She placed her hair behind her ears with both hands. "I'm not talking about a person who falls into sin and repents. It's the person who is content to live in sin and believe they are going to heaven. A simple head prayer without a heart transformation or metamorphosis is not salvation."

"Exactly!" Abigail said, nodding her head. "And anyone who stops doing righteousness and turns to a life of unrighteousness, all his righteousness will be forgotten. In other words, he will die in his sins." She gestured with both hands. "Anyway, I also found him coming out of a local motel with one of the nurses at the hospital." Her brown eyes teared. "That's why I'm here. How could I have been so deceived? How did I not see the first time he hinted at sin? How can a Christian not see the signs?"

"Because our flesh is weak, and we must deny self if we are to follow after Jesus."

"Amen!" Abigail said, rubbing her temples with the fingers of both hands. "My parents thought it was best for me to take a vacation, recognize the signs of sin, and gain wisdom for the future before starting my practice." She paused. "My father is the owner of Simpson Law Firm with a thousand lawyers each pulling in revenues of over a half million a year. He's setting me up in my own practice."

"This is unreal. I don't mean about your father's money. I meant about your experience. It seems all three of us came here for some healing. Isabelle's husband left her. I recently lost my mother, and I'm not sure if my fiancé is going to cancel our wedding." She touched Abigail's left arm. "You, too, have been injured by love."

"Yes, but thank God for his Holy Spirit that guides us into all truth. It is better to be injured in love than to sin against God."

Margaret giggled. "You seem like the kind of woman my fiancé's brother is looking for. He claims he will not marry until the Lord brings him a woman after God's own heart."

Abigail's face flushed. "No offense, although I have a lot of white friends, I feel my husband will be black."

"Oh my," Margaret said, giggling. "Titus is black. Joel's parents adopted him when he was eight and brought him from Liberia to America."

"They must be special people."

"None better. Their father is CEO at Schneider Wealth Management that he inherited from his maternal grandfather."

"Do you mean Jonathan Ryan?"

"Yes."

"What a small world. I remember my father stating what a high regard he had for one of his clients." Abigail gestured with both hands. "He said that Jonathan Ryan had adopted a boy from Liberia." She rubbed her temples with the fingers of both hands. "Anyway, I want a husband who obeys God's word."

Margaret nodded her head. "Like Joseph who resisted Potiphar's wife when she tried to seduce him." She took Abigail's right hand. "Lord, I thank you for bringing the three of us together. How selfish we can be at times in thinking we're the only one hurting. Help us to be a support to each other during this time of healing. In Jesus Name, Amen!"

"Amen!" Abigail said, sighing heavily. "Well, I think I'm going to go to the gazebo that's at the end of the east path and sit and pray. I came across it yesterday, and it's so peaceful. It sort of begs you to come in and pray." She looked at her watch. "Oh, my! I better get going or I'll run out of time. I'm booked for the medieval garden tonight after supper." She paused. "I'm not too pleased with the Hindu gods, but they are nothing more than man-made statues."

Margaret sat on the tree after Abigail left. She wondered how many Christians fail each other because they are so engrossed with their own problems. "Lord, how many times have I been insensitive to the hurting around me? How many times has my self-centeredness grieved your Holy Spirit?" Her eyes filled with tears. "Oh, Lord, help me to be more perceptive to your children who are engulfed in storms. I know my mother's death has had me self-centered and concerned about me and my pain. I've had spiritual tunnel vision when I should have had spiritual peripheral vision. Help me to be sensitive to what's going on in the lives of your children around me. Help me to be a light in their darkness."

"Amen!"

Margaret shrieked while spinning around to see Claudio standing there. "He touched Margaret's arm. I didn't mean to frighten you."

"I'm okay," Margaret said, breathing heavily. "I've been too uptight for some time now. I really need to rest in the Lord."

"As I was listening, I realized I've been guilty of that for too long. I wonder how many have come here hurting, and I was so engrossed in my unhappiness, that I did nothing to help?" He threw up both hands. "What is it with our selfishness? Why do we allow ourselves to be so self-centered? Why do we forget that we are to be light to others? We should be a lighthouse helping those out in the storm to find their way to safety."

Margaret nodded. "I believe the key is that we don't deny ourselves. Jesus said in order to follow him, we must deny self." She sighed, heavily. "If we're not denying self, we're not following Jesus."

"Whew! That's' a sobering thought."

Margaret gestured with both hands. "I thought you were going to read the book?"

"After hearing you talk about God's love being explained in chapter three, I decided to read it first." He sat on the log next to her. "That chapter not only enlightened God's love for me, but I truly didn't understand his forgiveness. I must have begged him thousands of times to forgive me for marrying Brenna." His eyes teared. "I knew she was an unbeliever. I knew we're not to be yoked with unbelievers." He shrugged his shoulders. "Although I repented, I guess I didn't believe God could forgive me for blatantly sinning against his word." He pulled the book out of his satchel. "Chapter three helped me to comprehend God's love, but it also illuminated God's forgiveness. When I repented, he immediately blotted out my transgression, and he will never use what he has forgiven against me. It's been the devil beating me with what God no longer holds against me." He paused. "Yes, my unhappiness has been the reaping of sowing. I chose a harvest of being out of God's will, and must reap what comes from being out of his will. But I wasn't reaping God's judgment, it was my planting the wrong seed." His voice choked with tears. "I heard his voice for the first time in years. He told me that he loved me and forgave me." He looked into Margaret's eyes. "I believe he's going to turn this around. I don't understand how, but I know I'm forgiven."

"I'm just in awe of what has happened in a few days, " Margaret said through glazed eyes. "I just found out that Abigail has also been injured by love."

"I saw her walking away as I was coming through the woods." He rubbed his left arm with his right hand. "The crazy thing is that Brenna wants nothing to do with me, but if she catches me talking to any of the female guests, she is downright nasty to them." He sighed, heavily. "I think she's concerned that I might be interested in one of them and divorce her." He shrugged his shoulders. "It's all insane. She knows my parents will never accept me divorcing her because she doesn't love me." He chuckled. "I know I've reaped what I sowed by marrying her, but there is such a release knowing God has forgiven me."

Margaret's face scrunched up. "Why would she be concerned about you talking to other women?"

"I sense she thinks that my parents might leave me everything when they die. She's obsessed with the properties. You see, she visited them both before we were married."

"That is so sad. She's so friendly to me. If I hadn't run into you, I would've believed you were this happy couple running this paradise."

Claudio put the book back in his knapsack. "I intend to finish reading this tonight in my room." He chuckled. "That's the one place I don't have to worry about Brenna entering." He stood up. "As matter of fact, she made sure my room was at the end of the castle far away from hers."

Margaret looked at her watch. "Well, I'm going to head to the canoes. It's almost dark. I may not have done bird watching today, but what a glorious day it has been."

"I better get back. Brenna expects me to bring in the wood for the fire place in the solar."

Margaret's face scrunched up. "The solar? What's that?"

"That's the private room where Brenna likes to get away to at night. No one is allowed in there. It's her place to read, sew, or whatever." He paused. "I was allowed there when we were first married. However, when my parents sent the letter disinheriting me, I was banned from the solar and our bedroom." He chuckled. "Now, I'm the servant who makes sure the fire is lit at night before she goes in there."

Margaret headed for the canoes and found herself skipping along the path. "Lord, I don't know why you didn't heal my mother, but I know she asked me to let her go." She stopped and gazed up at the sun going down. "I've been selfish in that also. As she was dying, she smiled and said she saw my father standing next to Jesus waiting for her." She burst into tears. "She missed him all those years to take care of me. How could I have been so self-centered?" She fell on her knees. "Lord, please forgive me for being angry at you for blessing my mother. I am so sorry. I know that your word says that if we ask anything according to your will, you hear us. And if we know that you hear us, whatever we ask, we know that we have the petition that we desired of you."

She stood up and reached into her pocket for her handkerchief. "Lord, it was your will for my mother to be reunited with my father." She said, blowing her nose. "If it had been your will to heal her, she would have been." She sighed, heavily. "How many times do Christians pray for something that's their will? Then, when it doesn't come about, they become angry with you?"

Margaret's legs stiffened and her body was ready to run at the sound of the leaves rustling to her left. Suddenly, a marmot or large ground squirrel stood up with a berry in its hands. She relaxed and giggled. "Lord, what is wrong with me? I seem to be acting like a fearful child afraid of the dark."

As she realized the moon was shining through the sky, she hurried to the canoes. She got into a canoe and decided to go upstream. While paddling, she heard various sounds of animals scampering through nearby undergrowth and wolves calling to one another. The moonlight seemed to cause the river to sparkle like a million diamonds. She was so mesmerized with the splendor of it that she hadn't realized how long she'd been out there. "Oh, my, I better get back. Supper is being served, it'll take me over an hour to get back, and I have to help Brenna clean up."

She started to paddle like she was trying to get away from a predator. Although she was aware of Brenna and Claudio's true relationship, she didn't want to give place for Brenna to catch on. Margaret determined to pretend she knew nothing and remain friendly with Brenna. Once she docked the canoe, she hurried to gather her belonging and head for the chateau. However, as she was walking back, she thought she heard a strange noise. She ducked down behind some bushes and looked towards the sound. Coming toward her direction was Blagdon pushing a wheelbarrow with a squeaky wheel. Margaret stayed hidden and peaked through the bushes. She gasped as the moonlight shone on what looked to be a motionless Abigail in the wheelbarrow. She felt her heart racing and tried to quiet her breathing.

After Blagdon passed, she decided to keep her distance and see where he was going. The noise of the wheelbarrow prohibited him from hearing any movement behind him in the distance.

He took her through unfamiliar paths. After sometime, he stopped, pulled a box out of an old oak tree, opened it, took out a key, and put it in his pocket. Then he walked towards the mountain and began to move away limbs, brush, and debris. Once finished, the moonlight revealed a hidden door. He put the key into the keyhole and opened it. Then it appeared that he unlocked another door inside.

Margaret was sure she heard crying or something coming from within.

She tried to get a better view, but Blagdon came out through the door. Immediately, she jumped back and didn't move. Apparently, he didn't hear anything because she heard him pushing the wheelbarrow in through the doors. She peaked to see what he was doing. After what seemed like hours, he pushed the empty wheelbarrow back out, locked the doors, went back to the tree, put the key in the box, put the box inside what looked like a hole in the tree, and headed back the way he came.

Margaret kept her distance and followed him back. He stopped at a gate outside the medieval garden, Brenna opened the gate. "That took you long enough."

"She seemed to be heavy or it's the wheel."

"You better get in. I'm still waiting for Margaret to come back."

He snickered. "She's tomorrow night. She doesn't seem to be heavy."

Brenna grabbed his right arm. "You'll do nothing with her." She gazed into his eyes. "Do you hear me?"

"You promised me all of them," he said, his jaw clenching. "She looks like she could be Janet's sister."

"She is not Janet, or anything like her." Brenna said, eyes glaring. "I said you'll do nothing to Margaret. You won't touch a hair on her head." She looked around. "Now, get in and do as I say."

Chapter Eight

The Hidden Cavern

MARGARET FELT HER INSIDES quaking. Should she run away? How would she help Brenna after what she heard? Did Brenna help Blagdon kill Abigail? She sat on the ground holding her head with both hands. "Lord, I need grace to know what to do. Do I go in as if nothing happened? How am I going to find out what's behind that door? If Blagdon catches me, he won't care what Brenna said."

She took a deep breath. "I can do all things through Christ which strengtheneth me." She got up and walked to the front entrance.

When she opened the door, Brenna was standing there. "You're late."

"I am so sorry. I didn't realize the time. When I did, I started to row back. Somehow, I got turned around in the woods." She slumped on the floor and broke into tears. "I thought I would never find my way back."

Brenna helped her up. "I was beginning to be quite concerned about you." She smiled. "Anyway, I'm glad you're safe." She gestured toward the Great Hall. "I've got your supper waiting." She put up her right hand. "I know what you said, but you are much too thin to go without eating. Especially with the nervous energy you've gone through tonight."

"I am quite hungry," Margaret said, sitting down at the table.

"While you're eating, I'll get all this into the kitchen. That will save us time in the clean-up."

Margaret prayed that Brenna wouldn't hear the racing of her heart as she helped her clean up. It was all she could do to carry on as normal when her body felt faint. She decided to just talk about what she's learned about the other guests. "It's strange how we can think we're the only ones going through things. As I heard Abigail and Isabelle talking about their troubles, I was ashamed how I've been since my mother's illness and death."

"What troubles?" Brenna said, her eyebrows squeezing together.

"First of all, Abigail's a doctor who fell for a doctor at the hospital where she finished her residence. She found him coming out of a motel with one of the nurses at the hospital." She sighed. "Isabelle's husband left her after five years of marriage for a woman in his business. It seems, he didn't want Isabelle to work even though she has a degree in business administration. He preferred to have his wife cook, clean, do laundry, etc." Her blue eyes widened. "It seems he wanted a maid and not a wife."

After Brenna heard about them, she seemed to be lost in her own thoughts. Her countenance took on a stony expression.

"Well, I guess I'll head for my bedroom," Margaret giggled. "We'll meet again in the morning."

"Brenna nodded her head. "I guess I'm quite done in tonight. I'll forego the solar and head for bed."

Margaret felt her whole body trembling as she headed for her bedroom, opened the door, hurried inside, and quickly locked it. She paced back and forth, as her mind raced with questions. She sat down on the chair near a small table in the corner of her room. "Lord, I must calm down. I can't allow fear to take me over." She grabbed her head with both hands. "We had to turn our cell phones off and leave them with Brenna when we arrived. We were told it's part of the rules to keep things quiet. If we have to use it, we must get permission from her." She rubbed the back of her neck with her right hand. "It will raise suspicion if I ask to use my phone."

All night Margaret kept hearing what seemed to be crying voices. Yet, Abigail hadn't moved. No matter how she tried, she couldn't fall into a deep sleep. Adrenaline spikes caused by fear and anxiety had her undone. She prayed that the Lord would help her overcome and lead her to solve the mystery revealed by moonlight.

She was up at the crack of dawn to make sure she was down for breakfast with everyone. When she entered the hall, only Claudio was there eating.

"Well, sleeping beauty is up early today," Brenna said, entering in from the kitchen.

Margaret took a seat at the other end of the table. She made sure to ignore Claudio. "Where is everyone today? I know I got up early enough."

Brenna poured Margaret a coffee. "Isabelle practically gobbled down her breakfast to get down to the river." She paused. "Abigail had some sort of family crisis. I received a phone call late last night. Anyway, Blagdon left about five to take her to the airport."

"That's about four hours away. I thought the limousine service meets about half way."

Brenna smiled. "Blagdon thought it would be quicker if he took her all the way." She paused, piling Margaret's plate with bacon, scrambled eggs, and hash browns. "It's really going to work out great. I needed some things in the town and Blagdon can kill two birds with one stone."

"Won't he be hungry?"

"He has a favorite restaurant near the airport that he'll take advantage of."

Margaret nodded her head and started to eat. "I can't believe how hungry I seem to be since I arrived here."

"It's the mountain air. When Blagdon and I came here as children, we couldn't get enough to eat for the longest of time." She glared at Claudio. "Don't you think you should get to work?"

Margaret looked down, pretending she heard nothing. She ate quietly while Claudio got up to leave.

He gestured with his right hand towards Brenna. "I have to take the truck into town for repairs today. I'll try to get back as soon as I can."

Brenna placed both hands on her hips. "Do whatever you have to do. As long as the solar is ready for me tonight."

After Claudio left, Brenna composed herself. "I think it's difficult for Claudio during this two weeks. He has to work like a servant." She threw up her hands. "I do believe we are all servants during this time." She smiled. "How else can the guests have the peace and quiet they pay for?"

Margaret giggled. "I don't know how any of you do it?" She stood up. "Well, at least I can be of help in the clean-up."

Margaret felt a shakiness in her limbs as she helped Brenna finish up. Her heart pounded so intense inside her chest that she felt it would pop out. Never had she been so frightened. She read plenty of suspense novels, but living one was most unnerving. She prayed she would be the protagonist that comes out victoriously through Christ.

Once outside, she ran to the spot where she heard the wheelbarrow the night before. She believed she could follow the tracks. Her mind raced. She would follow the tracks back out to the path. If she found the key, what would she find behind the doors? Is that where the bodies of the three women who disappeared last year are? She felt dizzy and her legs went limp. "Oh God, are there more than four bodies in there?" She said, holding a branch to stay up.

Gaining control, she proceeded to see where the tracks of the wheelbarrow entered the woods from the path. She was startled by a sound behind her. When she turned, it was Claudio. "What are you doing here? I thought you were going to the north woods today."

Margaret's legs went limp and she fell on her knees. "I came across something bizarre last night." She said, catching her breath. "I don't know how to tell you, but I think Blagdon murdered Abigail last night."

"W . . . what did you say?"

"I was coming back from canoeing when I heard a strange noise. I hid behind those bushes and saw Blagdon pushing a wheelbarrow. The moonlight revealed a motionless Abigail in it."

Claudio's legs went limp and he joined Margaret on the ground. "But Brenna said Blagdon is taking her to the airport because of a crisis or something."

"I know." She placed her hair behind her ears with both hands and pointed to tracks on the ground. "I believe following those tracks will lead us to what I believe is some sort of hidden cavern in the mountain." She stood up. "I saw Blagdon push the wheelbarrow with Abigail into it and push it back out empty."

"That must mean that Brenna knows about it."

Margaret nodded. "When I followed him back to a gate into the medieval garden, Brenna reprimanded him for taking so long." She gestured with her right hand. "He claimed Abigail was heavy."

Claudio took her hands into his. "Lord, give us the grace needed to see this thing through. We have no idea what we'll find. Help us to know what to do when we uncover what's in that cavern."

"Amen!" They said in unison.

Margaret and Claudio followed the tracks that appeared to stop at a bunch of bushes. Margaret looked around to find the tree she saw Blagdon pull out a box. "I believe this is the tree that I saw him pull out a box." She looked carefully and spotted a piece of rope. She pulled it up and the box was at the end of it. "This is the box," she said, opening it and taking out the key. "Here's the key." She pointed to the bushes. "Behind all that is a door."

They both began to clear it away. After a few minutes, they found the door. Margaret handed Claudio the key. "Here goes," he said, exhaling heavily. Once the door was opened, they stepped into a small opening revealing another door. Again Claudio put the key into the keyhole and opened the door.

Margaret screamed. "It's all lit up in here. What is this place?"

Claudio rubbed his right arm with his left hand. "It's a jail or something. Those are prison bars."

Abigail came running towards the bars. "Margaret! You found us! Praise God!" Behind her came three other women. One with long black hair that resembled Margaret, a short blue-eyed blond with curly hair, and a green-eyed brunette. Abigail pointed to each. "This is Janet Campbell, that's Sonya Kirkwell, and that's Jeanine Ferguson.

Claudio's eyes bulged. "Janet, Sonya, and Jeanine." He grabbed his head with both hands. "You've been imprisoned here since last year." He fell back against the wall. "When the police came, I confirmed that you all left."

Janet reached through the bars. "Claudio, how could you know what was done? Brenna and Blagdon had it all cleverly planned."

Margaret bit her bottom lip. "How do we get them out? Does that key fit the bars?"

Janet shook her head. "It seems there's something behind that door that closes the inner bars and opens these bars. Whenever our supplies are brought to us, we have to step over there, he closes those bars, and then opens these bars. If we don't do it, we get no supplies."

Claudio opened the door to see switches that read inner bars and outer bars. He switched the outer bars and they opened.

Abigail ran out and hugged Margaret. Then Janet, Sonya, and Jeanine did likewise. "How do we get them out of here without Brenna knowing?" Margaret said with tears streaming down her cheeks.

Claudio put his right hand up to silence her. "You take them down the river in the canoes, and I'll meet you at the landing. Brenna thinks I'm taking the truck into have it worked on." He paused. "However, we'll put everything back the way it was. I don't know how often Blagdon comes here."

"He brings us supplies on Saturday," Jeanine said. "Outside of last night, he has only come once a week since we've been imprisoned here."

"That's a relief. We'll not have to worry about him coming here today." Margaret said, sighing heavily."

Claudio reached into his satchel and pulled out his cell phone. "I'm going to call the gendarmerie and tell them to meet me at the landing."

Margaret's eyes squished together. "Who's that?"

Sonya smiled. "It's the police."

"May I use the phone after you call? I'd really like to call my fiancé and tell him what's going on." Margaret rubbed the back of her neck with her right hand. "Joel didn't have peace about the three women disappearing from here."

Chapter Nine

Sadness and Elation

AFTER MARGARET SPOKE TO Joel, he and Titus acquired permission from their father to use the company's Gulfstream G650. Joel kept quoting Isaiah 26:3 which says, *Thou wilt keep him in perfect peace, whose mind is stayed on thee: because he trusteth in thee.*

Titus put his right hand on Joel's left shoulder. "She'll be fine. I mean, after all, she discovered where the three missing women were imprisoned. Apparently, she and the other women were heading to meet up with the police down river. You must trust the Lord to protect her."

"I know the Lord will protect her, but I have this strange feeling that something bad is going to happen. I don't know what it is." His eyebrows squished together. "It's like this bad thing is really a good thing that must happen."

"Titus pulled his right eyebrow with his right thumb and forefinger. "I'm sensing it's how the Lord is going to work something out for good to those who love him."

"Yes! That's it." Joel scratched the back of his head with his right hand. "Now, we'll have to wait until we get there."

As Margaret, Claudio and the rest were heading to the path, Isabelle was heading their way. "I didn't know there were more guests coming," she said, stopping mid-stride. "Wait a minute! I thought Abigail had a family crisis or something and went back home?"

Margaret quickly gave her the details of what had happened the night before and how she knew Abigail hadn't left. "Anyway, after Claudio and I entered the hidden cavern, we found Abigail and the three women who disappeared last year."

"What are you going to do?" Isabelle said, grabbing Margaret's arm.

Claudio touched Isabelle's arm. "They're going to take the canoes down river to the landing. I'm going to meet them there with the police."

"Yes, I know the spot." She exhaled, heavily. "I do believe I'm joining you all in the canoes."

Margaret, Abigail, Isabelle, Janet, Sonya, and Jeanine paddled their canoes down the river heading for the landing. Margaret prayed that Claudio would have no trouble getting there. Her mind was in a whirlwind. Why did Joel seem so excited to hear her voice? She heard Titus say something in the background about the company jet. Were they going to come to France? What was this constant sense of foreboding? The women were all safe. "Lord, please protect Claudio. What if Brenna catches on?" She bit her bottom lip. "Why are the women all alive? I mean, I thank you they are. None of it makes sense to imprison them." Her blue eyes widened. "Lord, I am grateful they are alive. It was quite a shock to see Blagdon pushing a wheelbarrow with a motionless Abigail."

She was interrupted by Abigail shouting. "There's the landing. I see the police and Claudio waiting."

Margaret looked ahead. "Yes, I see them. Thank God!"

Abigail was the first to get to the landing followed by Margaret, Isabelle, Janet, Sonya, and Jeanine. They all hugged one another with tears strolling down their cheeks. Isabelle took Margaret's right hand in her hands. "If you hadn't seen what happened and followed Blagdon," she said, voice shaking, "we all would have ended up in that prison." She squeezed Margaret's hand. "But thanks be to God, which giveth us the victory through our Lord Jesus Christ."

As Janet stood on the landing, she fell to the ground as her emotions gave way. "I thought I was going to die in there."

Isabelle sat on the ground next to her. "God has other plans for you."

Janet looked into Isabelle's green eyes. "I was raised in the church, but I went my own way. What I did to Blagdon was horrible. I pretended to love him, but I thought I was marrying ownership in the chateau. When I found it was only Brenna who owned it, I skipped town." Her eyes filled with tears. "While in that prison, I prayed and asked the Lord to forgive me." She looked down at the ground. "I'm so ashamed that I doubted his existence." She gazed up as Margaret sat next to her. "Anyway, I told him if he delivered me that I would do whatever he wanted."

Claudio interrupted them. "I know this is all emotional, but we do have to get to the police station. This case has baffled many for a year."

"What will happen to Brenna and Blagdon?" Margaret said. "They both seem to be such pitiful people." She gestured with both hands. "Yet, what they have done is monstrous."

Claudio ran the fingers of his right hand through his brown curls. "With how publicized the disappearance of these three women was worldwide, they'll most likely receive the maximum punishment."

Margaret nodded her head. "What one sows, one will reap. Plain and simple."

"I just want to go home," Jeanine said, her chin trembling. "My parents are in their sixties. I'm an only child." She paused. "They must be beside themselves with worry. I've got to get home."

Sonya nodded. "I can't imagine what my husband and children have suffered." Her voice trembled. "I lost both my parents in an accident and Martin thought I needed to get away for a couple of weeks to talk to the Lord and heal. One of his associates at work had come here and told him about it." She paused. "I didn't want to leave them, but Martin said he was going to take the children in the RV to Dinosaur Valley State Park in Texas." Her shoulders drooped. "He thought that would help them to not miss me so much." She grabbed Margaret's right hand. "Getting back to my family is what kept me going the last twelve months. I don't know how I can ever thank you."

"If the Lord hadn't brought me to the chateau, if I hadn't been late paddling back, I would never have been where I was." Margaret squeezed Sonya's hand. "The Lord answered Janet's prayer by working it all out." Her eyes teared. "God does work all things together for good to those who love him."

Sonya hung her head. "I was too upset with the Lord for months to pray. About a month ago when I heard Janet praying, something hit me, and I broke. I asked the Lord to forgive me, and bring me back to my family."

"I guess it's confession time," Jeanine said, biting a hangnail on her right thumb. "My fiancé was finishing Bible College when his parents wanted to take him on a tour of Europe before we got married. They paid for me to come here." She gestured with both hands. "I pray he's still waiting for me."

Isabelle gave her a hug. "If he's sensitive to the Lord, he'll be waiting."

"He is sensitive to the Lord. I know that for a fact. He was ministering to people before he went to Bible college. He has an uncanny ability to know what people need to hear."

A Colonel Laurent handled the information given by the women. Janet, Sonya, and Jeanine were anxious about going home. They would come back for the trial. Arrangements were made for them to take the next flight home. Their testimonies were sufficient for the present. Of course, by the time they boarded their flight, it would be broadcast around the world.

The plan was for Margaret and Isabelle to paddle back up the river and be at the chateau for supper. Claudio would show up before them and let the Colonel know when Blagdon arrived. As soon as the police received a message from Claudio, the Colonel would come in the front entrance with Abigail.

Margaret and Isabelle prayed all the way to the chateau. Margaret decided that Isabelle should wait a few minutes before she entered the chateau. "Brenna has no idea that we even speak to each other. I told her I heard you and Abigail talking about why you were here." She paused. "I just didn't tell her you both talked to me." She gestured with her right hand. "Anyway, I'm not sure of what's going to happen, so we'll go in separately."

"That's right." Isabelle said, laughing. "As long as we can prevent our hearts from pounding out of our chest, all will be the same." She paused. "Thank God for his grace that is sufficient."

"Amen!"

When Margaret walked into the Great Hall, she found Claudio, Abigail, and the Colonel sitting at the table. "Where's Brenna?" Margaret asked.

"She's dead," Abigail said, choking back tears.

"What? How?"

Claudio motioned with his right hand. "As we were heading back here, Brenna's car was parked on the side of the road." He picked up a package. "The SAMU said she had a heart attack."

Margaret's face scrunched up. "The who?"

"It's the Urgent Medical Aid Service." He paused. "This package addressed to you upon her death was sitting on the passenger seat." He stood up, walked over to Margaret, and handed the package to her. "We were all waiting for you to see if it has any information that can help."

Margaret opened it and proceeded to look through the papers. She handed Claudio an envelope. "This letter is addressed to you." She continued going through the contents of the package. "Oh my!" Margaret said, pulling out a document. "This is her last will and testament." Her blue eyes bulged. "It's dated today." She unclipped an envelope attached to it.

Before she could read it, Claudio interrupted. "She asked me to forgive her for pretending to love me. She only wanted my parents property. It wasn't until she met Margaret that she saw what she had become. When her parents died, she turned on a God that could be so cruel. Her grandmother tried to convert her to Hinduism. But she figured if she lost faith in the God whose hands created the universe, she wasn't about to believe in gods made by human hands." His eyes watered. "She's asked the Lord to forgive her and prays I'll forgive her."

Margaret read her letter. "Brenna couldn't handle the girls being in the prison. She doesn't even know why she allowed Blagdon to do it. However, he wanted to murder them, but she would have no part of that." She bit her bottom lip. "But when I told her about Abigail and Isabelle's troubles, she knew it had to end. She understood Blagdon being upset with Janet, but did Sonya and Jeanine come for healing? Anyway, she went to the cavern to let the women out, found the prison empty, went to the canoes, saw them gone, and knew they had been discovered." She paused. "Apparently, she rushed to her lawyer to change her will, because she knew her heart wouldn't endure the stress of being arrested."

As Margaret spoke, her legs went limp. Isabelle had come in as Margaret began to speak and caught her fall. Claudio ran over to help. They both walked her over to a chair. After a few minutes, Margaret spoke through tears. "She claimed she loved me like a sister and wanted to thank me for my kindheartedness." Her blue eyes widened. "She has left me everything. I own the chateau, and she also put my name on her bank account and investments worth millions." She gazed at Claudio. "Brenna said the prenuptial agreement between you and her allowed her to leave everything to me."

Claudio nodded his head. "I wasn't marrying her for any property. I'm not after any of it." He gestured with both hands. "Perhaps, you could hire me to work here."

"I will do whatever I can to help you," she said, her voice shaking. "Her lawyer is to take care of the legal hassles because I'm a foreigner. He promised her to take care of everything to make the transition as easy as possible for me." She bit her bottom lip. "He will help me get naturalization after I've been here for five years." Her face scrunched up. "There's a bunch of stuff he'll help me with."

Abigail ran over and hugged Margaret. "That's wonderful. I mean," she said, clearing her throat, "not that Brenna's dead, but this place is like a paradise. The Lord has done so much healing here." She paused. "I do believe he'll do more with a child of his managing it."

Margaret rubbed the back of her neck with her right hand. "I don't believe I've ever experienced elation and sadness at the same time. I'm overwhelmed at being a woman of such wealth and overcome with grief at Brenna's death. I really became quite fond of her." She paused. "I never had any siblings, and she thought of me as sister. That's an incredible compliment."

Isabelle's eyes teared. "It's better to have fond memories of her than to hold animosity against her."

Margaret gestured towards the Hindu gods. "I want them and the statues in the garden out of here as soon as possible. Brenna told me she wished they weren't here, but she promised her grandmother to leave them."

"That's a terrific idea." Claudio said, rubbing his right arm with his left hand. "I've never been comfortable with false gods being displayed at each meal." He paused. "That's why I've stayed clear of the medieval garden. I felt devils were watching me the one time I did go in. It was most unsettling."

"Where's Blagdon?" Margaret said, rubbing the back of her neck with her right hand. "I would've thought he would be back by now."

The Colonel cleared his throat. "While we were heading here, I received a call. It seems earlier today, Blagdon was in a fatal accident." He shrugged his shoulders. "All we know is he had a blowout, swerved into the other lane of traffic, and was hit by a semitrailer. He died instantly." The Colonel stood up. "Well, I believe there's nothing else to find out." He looked at his watch. "My wife will have supper waiting for me." He shook everyone's hand. "I'll see my way out."

Chapter Ten

Revelation

As MARGARET WATCHED THE colonel leave, her eyes filled. "What a sad life. I didn't like Blagdon. When he looked at me, my skin crawled. But I wouldn't have wished any harm to him." Her blue eyes widened. "Of course, I had no idea that the women were imprisoned in that cavern or whatever it is." She slumped in her chair. "Brenna seems to have repented. She turned on God because of her parents death." She sighed, heavily. "I'm not sure if that's what I did after my mother's death."

Claudio nodded his head. "After her parents died, she turned on God. Both she and Blagdon wanted nothing to do with any deities." He stared down at his feet. "I do so wish I'd listened to my parents and my pastor. If I had, I could've avoided years of emotional pain."

Isabelle touched his right arm. "Negative consequences are always the result of being out of God's will."

"He gazed into Isabelle's green eyes. "Yes, but I chose to be out of his will. I thought I was in love with Brenna. In fact, it was the result of my fleshly lust." He gestured with both hands. "I knew my parents heard from the Lord, obeyed the Lord, and only wanted God's will for me. But I chose to disobey God's word. I knew Brenna didn't want to hear about God. In fact, she wanted nothing to do with him." He paused. "I don't know if I thought I could change her mind." He threw up his hands. "However, God will never honor sin. I blatantly sinned against God's will, and reaped what I'd sown."

Margaret put her long black hair behind her ears with both hands. "Yes, but when you repented, the Lord placed your sin as far as the east is from the west. He not only forgave you but forgot it." She bit her bottom lip. "He knew the day of your deliverance. Yes, it is sad, but you have made your peace with God." She paused. "You have your whole life ahead of you to pursue God's will."

Claudio took Isabelle's right hand between his hands. "Do you think you could be interested in someone who married out of God's will?"

She placed her left hand on his. "I do believe that I married out of God's will also. I just assumed that George was God's will because he went to church." She giggled. "What I mean, is do you think you could be interested in someone who believes she married out of God's will?"

They were interrupted by Claudio's phone ringing. As he pulled it out of his pocket, his hands trembled. "Dad, is this you?" He sat on a chair. "Yes, I'm fine. Yes, Brenna and Blagdon are both dead." He paused. "No, I'm not inheriting the chateau, she left it to a Margaret Anderson." He laughed. "Yes, she's the woman who discovered where Blagdon had the girls imprisoned." He sat back, tears strolling down his cheeks. "Yes, Dad, I'll be coming home as soon as I can." He sighed, heavily. "There's only one thing, I do believe I have someone for you to meet. She's a true woman of God. Her name is Isabelle Lefebvre-Duval."

He turned to Isabelle, covered his phone with his hand, and whispered. "Will you marry me?"

"Yes." Isabelle said, whispering.

"Anyway, Dad, we will be marrying there. If that's okay with you and Mom, we should be there as soon as we can catch a flight. Prayerfully it will be tomorrow or the next day. I have a few loose ends to finish up here." He paused. "I love you, Dad, and I have dearly missed you both."

Margaret and Abigail both ran to hug Isabelle and Claudio. "I'm so pleased for the both of you," Margaret said, giggling. "God is turning our lives around."

Abigail nodded. "He promises to work all things together for good to those who love him."

"Amen!" They said in unison.

Claudio laughed. "I don't know about the rest of you, but I'm extremely hungry. I don't know if there's anything prepared, but I think we should see about some supper."

Margaret, Isabelle, Abigail, and Claudio headed for the kitchen. Margaret paused. "This is my kitchen." She said, her voice choking with tears. "I'm in shock." She turned to Claudio. "I know you want to get home, but could you show me around this place? I mean, could you tell me what each room is? I know a little about castles through reading books, but not in experience."

He gestured with both hands. "I can do better than that. When we were first married, Brenna gave me a sort of blueprint of the place. It made it easy for me to learn my way around. Anyway, it has every room labeled, the paths, the grounds, and their function." He paused. "I'll get it for you after we get some food."

Isabelle held her stomach. "I hope you all don't hear this racket." She said, laughing. "We never stopped to have our lunch today. No wonder we're so hungry."

"Plus all the emotional stress, paddling down the river and the news that both Brenna and Blagdon have died." Abigail said, getting out the dishes to set the table."

There was a baked ham, a roasted turkey breast, a prime rib, vegetables, and deserts. Margaret heated up a spinach casserole, sliced some of the meat, grabbed some rolls, filled a serving tray, and started to carry it to the great hall.

Claudio took the tray from her. "I'll carry that in while you get us something to drink."

Isabelle took four glasses out of the cupboard and followed Claudio into the great hall.

Abigail perused the kitchen. "I think I'll bring that blueberry pie in."

Margaret nodded. "That sounds good. I'll see if there's any ice cream to go with it." She then checked the freezer and found some vanilla bean ice cream. "Here you go. That will top the pie quite splendidly."

"Yes, my lady." Abigail said, giving a belly laugh. "You are a true lady of the manor."

After Abigail exited the kitchen, Margaret took out a pitcher of iced tea from the refrigerator and carried it to the hall.

After they all sat, Margaret took Isabelle's right hand and Abigail's left hand. Isabelle took Claudio's right hand. Abigail reached across to Claudio's left hand. "Okay," Margaret said. "Claudio would you give thanks?"

"Wholeheartedly." He bowed his head. "Lord, I'm overwhelmed at your love, your forgiveness, and your blessings. Thank you for this manna that you've so bountifully supplied. Please nourish and bless it to our bodies and our bodies for service to you. In Jesus name, Amen?"

"Amen!" the women said in unison.

"Wow! I'm not sure what to think about all this." Margaret said, giggling. "I don't believe that I'm going back to the states." Her blue eyes widened. "I'll have to get someone to send some personal belongings, my clothes, and give my house to a Christian family with three children who go to my church." Her blue eyes widened. "I don't know where Brenna hid my cell phone."

Claudio stood up and walked away. When he came back, he had Margaret, Isabelle, and Abigail's cell phones. When Margaret looked at hers, she realized she had many missed calls and several text messages. As she went to look at the messages, she was interrupted by knocking at the door.

Abigail's face screwed up. "It can't be the police. I don't believe it's any guest." She stood up. "I'll answer it. I'm the closest to the door."

From the hall, Margaret heard Joel's voice. "We're looking for a Margaret Anderson."

"You must be Joel and that must be your brother, Titus." Abigail said, smiling.

Before he could answer, Margaret had run to the door. "Joel, Titus! What are you doing here?"

Joel ran to hug her. "Thank God you're safe."

Margaret's eyes teared. "I'm sorry for how I've been since my mother died." She took Joel's right hand and Titus's left hand. "Come in and meet everyone. We have some supper if you're hungry."

"I know I'm hungry." Titus said, giving a throaty laugh. "We left without any lunch. This has been one taxing trip."

Claudio stood up as they entered the hall. Margaret introduced Joel and Titus. "This is my fiancé, Joel Ryan and this is his brother, Titus Ryan." She then nodded towards Claudio. "That's Claudio Martinez. It was his wife who used to own the chateau." She then introduced Isabelle. "That's Isabelle Lefebvre-Duval who is recently engaged to Claudio." She gestured towards Abigail. "This is Dr. Abigail Simpson."

Titus pulled his right eyebrow with his right thumb and forefinger. "Doctor, impressive." He put out his right hand. "It's a pleasure to make your acquaintance."

They all shook hands and Joel and Titus joined them for supper. "This is quite a spread." Joel said, filling his plate with meat and spinach casserole."

Margaret put her long black hair behind her ears with both hands. "I think I have to let you know that I won't be going back to the states."

"What?" Joel and Titus said in unison.

"It seems I'm a woman of great wealth." She cleared her throat. "Brenna left me the chateau, all her money, and all her investments." Her blue eyes widened. "It's an enormous wealth."

Joel scratched the back of his head with his right hand. "You have to be kidding."

Abigail nodded her head. "She's telling the truth. It's all been left to her and not Claudio."

"I didn't doubt her," he said, his face flushing, "it's just that I spent the last couple of months trying to surprise her with a honeymoon in Italy. My father's secretary's parents own a chalet. I wanted to surprise her." He threw up his hands. "Now, she owns this place. She won't need to visit an Italian Chalet."

Isabelle gestured towards Margaret. "I told you Carlotta would not be trying to get your fiancé. It's not in her nature."

Joel's face blushed. "What?" He looked at Margaret. "You thought there was something between me and Carlotta?" He threw up his hands. "That's why you mentioned how pretty she was."

Titus gave a throaty laugh. "I told you it wasn't in Joel's nature either."

"I'm so sorry. It seems I was angry at God for taking my mother. That anger brought me farther and farther from truth. I started to imagine things." She rubbed the back of her neck with her right hand. "However, I know the note passing between you both was real." She gestured towards Titus. "He saw it too. But he was convinced there was a rational explanation." She paused. "He said I shouldn't doubt your faithfulness."

Joel hung his head. "Why didn't you tell me you saw the note passing? I thought we were being so discreet." He sat back in his chair. "Now, I find out Titus saw it too." He threw up his hands. "How many others thought something improper was going on?"

Claudio interrupted. "The main thing is that it's all straightened out. God has moved and blessed us all." His eyes teared. "I'm overwhelmed at his love, forgiveness, and mercy. My parents have forgiven me and want me to come home." He took Isabelle's right hand. "This beautiful woman has accepted my proposal of marriage, and we're heading to my parents' chalet in the Swiss Alps where we will be married and honeymoon at the Villa Hermosa that my parents own in Argentina."

"Wow!" Titus said, sitting back with folded arms. "How about Dr. Simpson. Do you own a chateau, chalet, or villa?"

"No, my father owns Simpson Law Firm."

Titus hit his head with his right hand. "That's why the name Simpson was familiar. They handle all our legal affairs."

Abigail blushed. "My father told me about your parents. He highly regarded them for adopting a young boy from Liberia." She gazed into his eyes. "God is a wonderful God! I have walked with him since I was ten. For the last twenty-three years, he has been so faithful."

"I've walked with him since I was eight. That's thirty years." He said, sighing. "He has been awesome."

"Excuse me!" Joel said, his eyebrows squishing together as he gestured towards Isabelle. "How do you know what Carlotta's nature is like?"

"We went to school together," she said, laughing. "We shared the same dorm and were quite close. People thought we were sisters." She paused. "Anyway, we lost contact after graduation, and she went back to Italy."

Joel took Margaret's right hand. "I know you said you're not going back to the states. However, we're still getting married next month, right?"

Margaret's eyes teared. "Yes." She paused. "I was thinking that cavern where the women were imprisoned seemed to become a house of prayer. God changed lives in there." Her blue eyes widened. "I'm going to convert that place into *The Mountain Chapel* and we'll be married in it." She gestured with both hands. "Surely it won't take long to have it ready."

Claudio clasped his hands. "I do talk to this minister now and again. His name is Reverend Marcus Shields who's from Texas. Well, he's told me many times he would love to have a place to preach. He moved here when his wife was dying about eight years ago to be next to her parents. He has no family left in the states."

"Praise the Lord!" Margaret said. "This way any guests we have can attend a service at the chapel when here."

Joel's eyebrows squished together. "I believe the Lord wants me to leave my father's business." He gazed at Titus. "It seems the Lord wants you to inherit our father's company." He laughed. "Of course, I'll expect you to vacation here with Margaret and me."

Titus hugged his brother. "I'll miss you, but yes, I'll be vacationing here." He gave a throaty laugh. "I do believe our parents will do likewise."

Chapter Eleven

Nightmare Hiding in Paradise

CLAUDIO SHOWED JOEL AND Titus to their bedrooms. "I guess we'll all meet at breakfast and do some planning." He shook their hands. "It's a pleasure to meet you both. I hope you'll be able to visit me. The chalet may not be intriguing unless you ski, but the villa is really something grand."

"Thanks be to God who always causes us to triumph in Christ." Joel said. "I'm so grateful to him for keeping Margaret safe."

"Amen!" Titus said.

Margaret was up early to make sure everyone had breakfast. She no sooner set everything out when Claudio, Joel, Titus, Abigail, and Isabelle entered the hall. "I'm starving," Titus said, giving a throaty laugh."

Joel sat down. "I smelled food cooking upstairs. My stomach growled, so I went to Titus's room and woke him up."

They all started to fill their plates, while Margaret poured everyone a coffee. When she finished, she took her seat next to Joel. "Claudio, when will the staff be back? You said there is a full staff."

He sat back in his chair. "I think you'll have to call each of them. I'm sure they've heard the news and won't think they have a job any longer." He gestured with his right hand. "Brenna kept all the information in a room off her bedroom. She called it her private office. After we eat, I'll show you to her room. You can check out her office and get their names." He rubbed his right arm with his left hand. "As a matter of fact, if you're not superstitious, that is the main bedroom of the chateau." He hesitated. "If you don't mind me interfering, there are three women who are quite lazy. I don't know why Brenna kept them on." His face screwed up. "Wait a minute! Now that I think of it, they were all gone the day the three women were to fly home. All they would have to do is pretend they were Janet, Sonya, and Jeanine." He grabbed his head with both hands. "As a matter of fact, Mable resembles Janet in size. A wig would have fooled anyone who didn't know Janet. Teresa resembles Sonya in size and hair color. Rhonda resembles Jeanine in size. A wig would have sufficed for her."

Abigail laughed. "How were they going to pull my disappearance off?"

"All Rhonda would have to do is use some color to darken her skin. She is about your size and shape."

"That incredible." Titus said. "What wickedness." He gestured with his right hand. "What was the purpose of the imprisonments?"

Margaret cleared her throat. "Brenna repented of everything and said Blagdon wanted to kill them. She would have no part of murder. As a matter of fact, she didn't know why she even went along with him on the imprisonment."

"Thank God you came here." Isabelle said, sighing.

Margaret's blue eyes widened. "I think we have more information for the Colonel to do some investigating to see if those women took a flight back here."

Titus pulled his right eyebrow with his right thumb and forefinger. "Let's put this wickedness behind us." He gave a wide grin. "I'd like to check this place out." He gave a throaty laugh. "I must admit this is quite the place. After breakfast, I'd like to peruse the land."

Abigail leaned forward. "Let me tell you this place is like walking through paradise. It's such a peaceable atmosphere." She paused. "I found this gazebo at the end of the east path that's almost supernatural. When I sit in there and pray, I'm instantly in the presence of the Lord."

Margaret nodded. "When I arrived, I was overwhelmed with the peace and serenity. The Lord has given me such a healing here." Her eyes filled with tears. "I was angry at God for blessing my mother. Before she died, she told me she saw my father standing next to Jesus waiting for her."

Joel's eyebrows squished together. "You never told me that."

"I guess I was too upset with God for not healing my mother that I couldn't see he was blessing her."

Claudio interrupted. "Margaret let me show you that room right after you finish eating." He put up his right hand. "Seeing I'm finished, let me get that blueprint for you." He hurried out of the hall.

Isabelle sat back in her chair. "I'm quite excited about meeting Claudio's parents. We'll be leaving this evening. He booked our flight last night." She paused. "Claudio said he'll get his things packed and drop them off to be shipped to his parents. Then we'll catch the flight out of here." She smiled. "Prayerfully, we'll be married the following Saturday and head for the villa in Argentina for a couple of weeks. After that, we'll be working the chalet with his parents."

Claudio interjected. "My parents usually spend the winter months in Argentina while Hans Rhyner manages the chalet for them. He's getting up in years, but he's to help them run the villa when they retire there. They want to get away from the cold weather. Now, they can devote their time to the villa, and we'll run the chalet." He handed the blueprint to Margaret. "This outlines everything quite well. Brenna has some more copies in her office." He gave her back her book. "Again, thank you for allowing me to read this book." He looked down at his feet. "Chapter five says every storm that hits us, no matter how suddenly it comes, Jesus is by our side to give the strength of faith to outlast the storm. It's us who take our eyes off him and concentrate on the storm." He threw up his hands. "I forgot that Jesus will never leave nor forsake me. I forgot his presence was with me. I tried to go it alone, when he was waiting for me to ask for his help."

"I think I was doing the same." Margaret said, rubbing the back of her neck with her right hand."

Titus gestured towards Abigail. "I'd like to visit that gazebo you talked about."

Abigail finished her coffee. "I can take you there now."

After Titus and Abigail left, Claudio and Isabelle both stood up. "I don't have much to pack," Isabelle said, giggling.

"I really don't have that much either," Claudio said, rubbing his right arm with his left hand. "However, I'm really relieved to be leaving here." He paused. "It's not that I disliked the place, it's just that what I thought was wonderland turned out to be a nightmare hiding in paradise."

Joel rubbed the back of his neck with his right hand. "Thank God that nothing is secret, that shall not be made manifest; neither anything hid, that shall not be known and come abroad." He paused. "It must have really been a nightmare hiding in paradise to those three women imprisoned for a year."

Margaret bit her bottom lip. "Yes, but paradise wasn't the nightmare, it was malevolence in people." She touched Joel's right hand. "God has pulled away the cloak hiding the nightmare and brought it to light." She got up. "Thank God, it will once again be a paradise of peace and tranquility for all guests in the future."

"Amen!" They all said in unison.

www.ingramcontent.com/pod-product-compliance
Lightning Source LLC
Chambersburg PA
CBHW071315200626
46813CB00015B/2210